MR. SILVER
and
MRS. GOLD

by

Dale Borman Fink

illustrated by Shirley Chan

HUMAN SCIENCES PRESS
72 Fifth Avenue   3 Henrietta Street
NEW YORK, NY 10011 ● LONDON, WC2E 8LU

Library of Congress Cataloging in Publication Data

Fink, Dale B
    Mr. Silver and Mrs. Gold.

    SUMMARY: Two old people become friends and share
many activities together.
    [1.   Old age—Fiction.   2.   Friendship—Fiction]
I.   Title.
PZ7.F49575Mi   [Fic]   LC 79-15924
ISBN 0-87705-447-9

*To the memory of
my Grandpa, William Borman*

Mr. Silver was a very old man who lived all by himself.

Mrs. Gold was a very old woman who lived all by herself.

Mr. Silver was lonely. He had no one to drink coffee with, no one to listen when he played his harmonica, and no one to work with in his garden.

Mrs. Gold was lonely too. She had no one to sip tea with, no one to listen when she played her piano, and no one to share her homemade bread.

One day Mr. Silver was taking his cat for a stroll in the park.

The same day, Mrs. Gold was taking her dog for a walk in the park.

Mr. Silver got very tired and sat down to rest.
Mrs. Gold got very tired and sat down to rest.

"Hello," said Mr. Silver.
"Hello," said Mrs. Gold.
"My name is Mr. Silver," said Mr. Silver.
"My name is Mrs. Gold," said Mrs. Gold.

"I live just up the street," said Mr. Silver.
"I live just down the street," said Mrs. Gold.
Mr. Silver smiled at Mrs. Gold.
Mrs. Gold smiled at Mr. Silver.
"See you later, Mrs. Gold."
"See you later, Mr. Silver."

After that, Mr. Silver and Mrs. Gold saw each other at the park almost every day.

One day Mr. Silver asked Mrs. Gold, "Would you like to come up to my house for a cup of coffee?"

"Oh, heavens!" said Mrs. Gold. "I'd love to. But I never drink coffee. It's too bitter. Would you like to come down to my house for a cup of tea?"

"Oh, pity!" said Mr. Silver. "I'd like to. But I never sip tea. It's too sour."

They went to a little sandwich shop around the corner. Mr. Silver ordered a cup of coffee, with sugar and cream. Mrs. Gold ordered a cup of tea, with honey and a slice of lemon.

Mr. Silver drank his coffee and smiled at Mrs. Gold.
Mrs. Gold sipped her tea and smiled at Mr. Silver.
"See you soon, Mrs. Gold."
"See you soon, Mr. Silver."

After that, Mr. Silver and Mrs. Gold went to the sandwich shop
together almost every day.

One day Mrs. Gold asked Mr. Silver, "Would you like to come down to my house and hear me play my piano?"

"Yes," said Mr. Silver, "But first let me go up to my house and get my harmonica."

So Mr. Silver and Mrs. Gold walked up the street to Mr. Silver's house to get his harmonica. Then they walked down the street to Mrs. Gold's house.

Mrs. Gold sat down and played her piano.

Mr. Silver stood up and played his harmonica.

"The piano sounds beautiful," said Mr. Silver.

"The harmonica sounds wonderful," said Mrs. Gold.

Mr. Silver and Mrs. Gold smiled at each other.

"See you tomorrow, Mrs. Gold."

"See you tomorrow, Mr. Silver."

After that, Mr. Silver and Mrs. Gold played music together almost every day.

One day Mr. Silver asked Mrs. Gold, "Would you like to come up to my house for lunch? The vegetables are ready to be picked from my garden. We could have a nice salad."

"Yes," said Mrs. Gold. "But first let me go down to my house and get a fresh loaf of bread that I baked last night."

So Mr. Silver and Mrs. Gold walked down the street to Mrs. Gold's house to get the homemade bread. Then they walked up the street to Mr. Silver's house. They picked lettuce and cucumbers and tomatoes and carrots from his garden. Mr. Silver made a lovely salad.

Then they sat down for lunch.
"This bread sure is tasty!" said Mr. Silver.
"These vegetables sure are tender!" said Mrs. Gold.

"I wish I could bake bread like this," said Mr. Silver.
"I'll teach you," smiled Mrs. Gold.

"I wish I could grow vegetables like these," said Mrs. Gold.
"I'll teach you," smiled Mr. Silver.

After that, Mrs. Gold spent many mornings in Mr. Silver's yard,
learning how to grow vegetables. Mr. Silver spent many afternoons in
Mrs. Gold's kitchen, learning how to bake bread.

Sometimes when he was at Mrs. Gold's house, Mr. Silver sipped tea. With honey and a slice of lemon, it wasn't as sour as he expected.

Sometimes when she was at Mr. Silver's house, Mrs. Gold drank coffee. With cream and sugar, it wasn't as bitter as she expected.

One day Mr. Silver said to Mrs. Gold, "You know, my house is big enough for two. Maybe you should move in with me."

Mrs. Gold frowned. "What about my piano? We would never be able to move my piano."

The next day Mrs. Gold said to Mr. Silver, "You know, my house is big enough for two. Maybe you should move in with me."

Mr. Silver frowned. "What about my garden? You know we can't move my garden."

"But we could plant a new garden in my yard," Mrs. Gold suggested. "How about that?"

"No, thank you," said Mr. Silver. "I have spent so many happy years in my house. I want to stay there."

"But we could pay somebody to move your piano to my house," Mr. Silver suggested. "How about that?"

"No, thank you," said Mrs. Gold. "I have spent many happy years in my house, too, and I want to stay there."

Mr. Silver laughed and put his arms around Mrs. Gold.
Mrs. Gold laughed and put her arms around Mr. Silver.

"I'm glad you live just down the street from me, dear Mrs. Gold."
"And I'm glad you live just up the street from me, my dear Mr. Silver."

Mr. Silver still lives by himself.
Mrs. Gold still lives by herself.

But now Mr. Silver has someone to drink coffee with, someone to
listen when he plays his harmonica, and someone to work with in
his garden.

Mrs. Gold has someone to sip tea with, someone to listen when she
plays her piano, and someone to share her homemade bread.

Mr. Silver and Mrs. Gold are not lonely anymore.